W9-DAU-282

Werewolves Don't Go To Summer Camp

by
Debbie Dadey and Marcia Thornton Jones

illustrated by John Steven Gurney

Scholastic Inc.

New York Toronto London Auckland Sydney
Mexico City New Delhi Hong Kong Buenos Aires

To our parents, for keeping the
werewolves away

                                        D.D. and M.T.J.

If you purchased this book without a cover, you should be aware that this
book is stolen property. It was reported as "unsold and destroyed" to the
publisher, and neither the author nor the publisher has received any payment
for this "stripped book."

No part of this publication may be reproduced, stored in a retrieval system,
or transmitted in any form or by any means, electronic, mechanical,
photocopying, recording, or otherwise, without written permission of the
publisher. For information regarding permission, write to Scholastic Inc.,
Attention: Permissions Department, 557 Broadway, New York, NY 10012.

ISBN-13: 978-0-590-44061-5
ISBN-10: 0-590-44061-6

Text copyright © 1991 by Debra S. Dadey and Marcia Thornton Jones.
Illustrations copyright © 1991 by Scholastic Inc.
All rights reserved. Published by Scholastic Inc. SCHOLASTIC,
APPLE PAPERBACKS, THE ADVENTURES OF THE BAILEY
SCHOOL KIDS, and associated logos are trademarks and/or
registered trademarks of Scholastic Inc.

84 83 82 81 80 79 78 77 76 75 74 73   13 14 15 16 17 18 19 20

Printed in the U.S.A.   40

This edition first printing, July 2007

1

The New Camp

"I'm scared," Liza whispered.

Melody rolled her brown eyes. "Camp won't be so bad."

A new summer camp had been formed close to Bailey City. All the parents thought the week-long camping program was a great idea, and practically every kid from the second and third grades at Bailey Elementary School had been signed up for the first session. They were all on a big green bus taking them to the camp.

"What's the worst thing that could happen?" Howie's freckled face peered over the seat in front of them.

Liza's eyes got wide. "I could get lost in the woods and be eaten by wild animals."

1

"Only if we're lucky," Eddie teased from the seat behind them.

Melody ignored him. "Don't worry, Liza, there aren't any wild animals around here. And if you get lost in the woods, I'll make everyone look for you no matter how long it takes."

"But what if we both get lost together?" Liza asked.

"Don't be stupid. I'm not going to get lost anywhere." Melody squeezed her legs together. She had needed to go to the bathroom ever since they'd left the school parking lot. There was a bathroom on the bus, but Melody didn't want to use it.

Liza tapped Melody on the arm. "I'm carsick."

"Well, don't puke on me." Eddie pulled his T-shirt over his red curly hair.

Melody felt a little sick herself, but she'd seen Liza throw up on too many

2

school trips to ignore her. "Stick your head out the window and you'll feel better," Melody said quickly.

Liza had just poked her head out the window when she hollered, "I see the sign for the camp. We're almost there."

"Thank goodness," Melody said. She wasn't thrilled about going to camp either. But at the moment there was nothing that would make her happier than a nonmoving bathroom.

All the kids strained to read the sign as the bus pulled onto the gravel driveway. It read *Welcome to Camp Lone Wolf.*

2

Mr. Jenkins

Eddie was out the door of the bus almost before the wheels stopped moving. He never could wait for anything.

All the other kids piled out after him. But not Melody or Liza.

"Come on, Liza," Melody urged. "I've got to go."

"I'm scared," Liza whined. "I've never been here before."

"None of us have," Melody snapped. "It's a brand-new camp."

"What if the camp counselors are mean? For all we know, they could be escaped convicts!"

Melody rolled her eyes. "Well, you can sit here all day if you want, but I have to go and I'm going now!" With that she grabbed her blue Bailey School gym bag and headed for the door.

Liza sure didn't want to be alone, so she clutched her gym bag and followed Melody.

"All right, you city slickers," boomed the loudest voice they'd ever heard. "Line up against that bus and listen for your cabin assignments."

"But sir," Melody raised her hand, "I need to—"

"You need to listen. Now button up," growled the man.

Howie pulled Melody back against the bus. "Shhh. This guy means business."

"I'm gonna do some business if he doesn't hurry!" Melody said through clenched teeth.

"My name is Mr. Jenkins," the man interrupted. His voice was loud enough for their parents to hear back in Bailey City. "I'm your camp director, so if you need anything, let me know."

"I need to go to the bathroom," Melody hissed under her breath.

"Where'd they find this nut?" Howie whispered.

"He's probably a reject from the Marine Corps," Eddie said.

"Yeah, a berserk drill sergeant," snapped Melody.

Howie nodded. "He *is* wearing dog tags."

"Shhh," Liza warned. But it was too late. Mr. Jenkins turned and glared in their direction.

"No talking in the ranks," he bellowed as he scratched his black beard, causing the tags around his neck to jingle. "Anyone who doesn't want to hear their cabin assignment can sleep outside with the wolves!"

Something about Mr. Jenkins made you listen to him. He was at least six and a

half feet tall and looked like a professional football player. His brown Camp Lone Wolf T-shirt was tight across his huge chest, and the silver dog tags hung from his thick neck. He had the kind of arms that could break a kid in half like a toothpick. His blue jeans were faded to almost white, and he wore no shoes, even though it was a chilly afternoon. But the thing that the kids noticed most was his hair.

Mr. Jenkins had hair everywhere. There was enough hair on his head for three people, and his thick beard would have made five bald men happy. Even his arms were covered with a forest of black hair.

Everyone quieted down as he called out the cabin assignments. Eddie and Howie ended up together in Cabin Silver Wolf along with six other boys from Bailey City. Luckily, Melody and Liza were both put in Cabin Gray Wolf. Melody rushed ahead of the other girls and made it to the bathroom just in time.

When Melody came out of the bathroom, the other girls had already picked out their beds. The only one left was the bunk over Liza's.

"Liza, I'll trade you," Melody said lightly.

"No, I can't sleep that high. I'd get sick and throw up all over you."

"Some choice," Melody complained. "Either I sleep in the nosebleed section, or I get puked on."

After everybody settled in their cabins it was time for dinner. Mr. Jenkins was grilling hamburgers outside.

Howie and Eddie put their plates on the picnic table and sat down next to Liza and Melody.

"What's wrong with you?" Howie asked Melody.

"Twitter brain there is making me sleep on the top bunk." Melody glared at Liza.

"I'll probably fall off and break my neck!"

"But I don't like the top bunk," Liza whined. "It makes me sick to look over the edge."

"I like the top bunk," Howie told Melody. "I think it'll be fun!"

"I think it'd be more fun to go home and get out of this place," mumbled Eddie with his mouth full of cold hamburger. "Yuk! These aren't even cooked." Eddie squeezed his hamburger. Red juice oozed onto the plate, leaving a puddle.

"Ew, that looks like blood." Liza gulped.

"I can't eat raw meat!" Howie exclaimed. "I'm going to see if Mr. Jenkins will cook mine a little longer."

The rest of the kids agreed. They all carried their rare beef to where Mr. Jenkins was grilling more hamburgers.

"Excuse me," Howie said softly. "But our burgers aren't quite done."

Mr. Jenkins glanced at the juicy beef

and licked his lips. "Looks done to me," he said. "I like my meat rare." He grabbed Liza's burger from her plate and took a huge bite. Juice oozed from the corners of his mouth and dripped down his black beard.

"Nothing wrong with this meat," he said, licking the juice with his tongue.

Howie, Liza, and Melody went back to their seats without saying a word. None of them felt hungry anymore. Even Eddie, who usually made a smart remark about everything, was quiet as he sat down.

"I think Mr. Jenkins is strange," Howie said.

Eddie nodded. "Anybody who eats raw meat must be part animal!"

"He's hairy enough to be an animal," Liza said.

Melody laughed. "He has more hair than a wolf in winter."

"Maybe he is a wolf." Liza giggled.

"Yeah, a werewolf," Eddie added.

"Oh, there are no such things as were-wolves," Howie said.

"Sure there are," Eddie teased. "I bet Mr. Jenkins is one and he comes out at midnight for a snack. He likes to eat raw campers, especially ones named Liza!"

"Quit it, Eddie," Melody fussed. "You're scaring Liza."

"A flea could scare her," Eddie laughed.

"It could not! Besides, werewolves aren't for real," Liza said. "Are they?"

3

The Legend

"This is creepy," Liza whispered. "It's already getting dark."

Melody sighed. "You'd think a bright day was creepy."

The counselors and campers were sitting around a huge campfire. That is, all of the counselors but one. Mr. Jenkins sat back a little from the fire. In the fading light, Melody could barely make out their camp director's Camp Lone Wolf T-shirt and his hairy face. It was hard to believe he still wasn't wearing shoes even though it was a bone-chilling night.

"What's wrong with Mr. Jenkins, anyway?" Melody asked. "Why isn't he sitting with everyone else?"

"He *is* kind of weird," Liza agreed.

"From the way he acts, you'd think he was afraid of the fire instead of the dark."

Just then Mr. Jenkins began to speak. "This is your first night at Camp Lone Wolf, and I suppose some of you might be homesick. But we'll have no crybabies at this camp." His big toothy grin sent chills up all the campers' backs.

Liza shuddered. "He sure is mean."

"Shhh," whispered Melody.

Mr. Jenkins glared at them. His eyes gleamed from the firelight. "By the end of this week you'll be experienced campers, able to take care of yourselves in the wilderness."

Eddie never did know when to be quiet. "But Mr. Jenkins, we don't need to know how to live in the wilderness. We all come from Bailey City!"

Mr. Jenkins scratched his thick black beard. "You never can tell when a little kid like you might get stranded in the

woods." Eddie didn't say another word as Mr. Jenkins continued. "There's a local legend about just such a boy who wandered away from a campfire."

"Was it at this camp?" Howie asked.

"No, it was long ago, even before Bailey City was founded. The boy's family was moving west. They were camping in this area when he strayed from the campsite. They searched for that boy for three weeks, but they never did find hide nor hair of him. He simply disappeared into thin air. Except for . . . "

"Except for what?" Liza squeaked.

Mr. Jenkins glanced at the faces around the campfire. "Well, it's probably only a coincidence, but ever since he disappeared, the howling of a lone wolf can be heard in these woods. A howling that had never been heard before."

Liza dug her fingernails into Melody's

arm. "Did the wolf eat the boy?" she asked.

Mr. Jenkins slowly shook his head. "No one knows. But on certain nights, especially when there's a full moon, that wolf can still be heard. That's how this camp got its name."

A few kids looked up nervously. The sky had suddenly darkened as heavy clouds covered the nearly full moon.

"I bet you're just trying to scare us," Eddie cried. "There aren't any wolves around here!"

Mr. Jenkins scratched his beard and stared at Eddie. "If you're so sure, why don't you sleep outside tonight? The rest of you better head for your bunk beds. Sleep well, if you can!"

One of the camp counselors covered the flames with dirt while the campers headed to their cabins.

"Are you gonna do it?" Howie asked

Eddie. "Are you going to sleep outside?"

"Naw. Mr. Jenkins is just trying to scare us," Eddie said.

"Why would a grown man try to scare a bunch of kids?" Liza asked.

"Because he's a wolf," Melody whispered. "I bet he's a werewolf!"

They all jumped as a flash of lightning streaked across the sky, and thunder rumbled in the distance.

By the time everyone arrived at their cabins they were soaking wet.

"Gee, it's really coming down in buckets," Eddie sputtered.

Howie dumped water out of his sneakers. "It's a good thing you don't have to sleep outside tonight."

"Sleeping outside doesn't scare me!" Eddie boasted.

"What about the wolf?" Howie asked.

Eddie stretched out on his bunk. "You don't believe that stupid legend, do you?"

"I don't know. Mr. Jenkins is awfully hairy. . . . He just might be a werewolf."

Eddie rolled his eyes. "There are no wolves around here. And there is no such thing as a werewolf."

"Well, if you're so sure, why don't you sleep outside like Mr. Jenkins said?"

"In this rain?" Eddie gasped. "I'd drown!"

"Then do it tomorrow night," Howie dared. "If you're really not scared, you will!"

"I'm not scared," Eddie declared. "I'll do it!"

Huge bolts of lightning cut through the night sky, and thunder boomed. Eddie and Howie both jumped as the lights flickered, then went dead.

With the lights out there wasn't much anybody could do but go to sleep. The cabin counselor lit lanterns while everybody put on their pajamas.

* * * * *

Over in Cabin Gray Wolf, the girls got ready for bed by lantern light, too. When all the girls were in their bunks, and the lanterns were turned out, the girls found out what dark really was. Melody couldn't even see her hand in front of her face until there was a flash of lightning. She was just starting to get drowsy when Liza whispered her name.

"Melody, can I sleep with you?"

"I thought you were scared of the top bunk," Melody said into the darkness.

Liza hoisted herself onto Melody's bed. "Please? I'm more scared of the dark."

"Oh, all right." Melody sighed and squeezed over to one side of the tiny bed as Liza snuggled down under the covers.

Melody was too crowded to sleep so she stared out the window beside her bed.

A lantern from another cabin cast an

eerie glow on the nearby trees. Thunder rumbled in the distance. The rain pounding on the roof nearly put her to sleep. Melody's eyes shot open just as a bolt of lightning cut through the sky. The light was so bright, she could see the hunched figure of a hairy beast dashing into the woods.

Melody grabbed Liza's arm. "Did you see that?"

"Leave me alone," Liza muttered. "I'm trying to sleep."

"Liza!" Melody cried as she shook her friend. "I saw it, I saw it!"

"Saw what?" Liza mumbled sleepily.

"The wolf," Melody whispered into the darkness. "I saw the lone wolf. And it was wearing dog tags!"

4

Dead Man's Float

"It was after the lights went out and everyone else was asleep," Melody said at breakfast the next morning. "I saw a wolf creature run into the woods."

"Aw, you were just dreaming," Eddie sneered as he crunched on some bacon.

"I really did see it," Melody insisted. "Didn't I, Liza?"

"Maybe it *was* just a dream," Liza said softly. "I didn't see anything."

"It was kind of spooky when the lights went out," Howie added. "Maybe you just imagined it."

"I did not. I really saw a wolf!" Melody looked like she was ready to cry.

"There *is* no wolf!" Eddie snapped. "And I'm gonna prove it tonight."

Melody's face grew pale as she opened her mouth to speak. But she never got the chance.

"Prove what?" growled Mr. Jenkins as he walked up behind Eddie.

The campers peered up at their camp director. He had dark circles under his eyes as if he hadn't slept all night. He still wore his Camp Lone Wolf T-shirt, faded jeans, and dog tags. His hair was tangled, and his beard seemed even bushier than yesterday.

Howie finally broke the silence. "Oh, Eddie's just kidding around. It was nothing, really."

Mr. Jenkins rubbed his beard and turned away. "Everybody into their swimsuits," he yelled.

Liza whimpered, "But I don't know how to swim."

"You don't know how to do anything," Eddie sneered.

Mr. Jenkins faced Liza. "Swimming lessons are free. Besides, you need to learn. Only the fittest survive in the wilderness! And swimming is an excellent way to stay fit." Mr. Jenkins reached out and pinched Liza's plump arm. "And it looks like you need some exercise," he added.

After changing into their bathing suits, the campers met on the dock at the lake. Mr. Jenkins was already there.

Eddie poked Howie in the arm. "Look at the hair on Mr. Jenkins."

Howie had already noticed. As a matter-of-fact, all the campers were staring at Mr. Jenkins. Black curly hair crept all the way up his arms and over his shoulders. He had more hair on his chest and back than most dogs.

"I've never seen so much hair in my life," Melody whispered. "And he's still wearing those dog tags!"

Mr. Jenkins silenced their whispers with a single look before jumping into the water. "Everybody in," he growled from the water. "You'll never learn the dead man's float standing on the dock."

Some of the campers stuck their toes in, as if they were testing their bathwater. But Eddie didn't budge.

"The water is too cold," he said just loud enough for everyone to hear. "It'll wrinkle my fingers."

"And it's way too deep," Liza added. "I might sink."

Mr. Jenkins' eyes looked like slits as he squinted into the sun. Then he started to swim to the dock. He didn't swim like most grown-ups. Instead, he kept his head high above the water.

"Look at that," Melody hissed. "He's doing the dog paddle!"

Mr. Jenkins pulled himself onto the dock in front of Eddie, Liza, Howie, and

Melody. Water dripped down his legs and formed a puddle around his feet. Mr. Jenkins licked the water from his mustache. Then, starting with his belly, he began to shake, spraying the campers with water.

Liza grabbed Melody. "He's acting just like a dog."

"Or a wolf," Melody added.

Mr. Jenkins finished shaking. He scratched his beard and looked straight at the campers. "You *will* get in, or I'll teach you the dead man's float the hard way."

"How's that?" gulped Liza.

"Get in, or you'll find out," growled Mr. Jenkins.

Liza backed away from the dripping Mr. Jenkins.

"Be careful," Howie whispered. But it was too late. Liza took one step too many and fell off the dock. She came up splashing like the Loch Ness monster, swallowing almost a gallon of lake water.

"Help me," she gasped. "I'm drowning."

Eddie didn't think twice. He jumped in to rescue her, but Liza just climbed on top of his head, pushing him underwater.

"Help!" she screamed.

Mr. Jenkins splashed into the lake beside them.

"Save me! Save me!" Liza wailed.

Mr. Jenkins scooped up Liza with a big hairy arm and held her high above the water.

Eddie popped his head above the surface and spurted out a stream of water. "Were you trying to kill me?" he screamed.

"But I was drowning," Liza sniffed.

"You moron. This water only goes up to our belly buttons!" Eddie stood up to prove his point.

Liza's face turned bright red. "Oh," was all she could say as she wiped away a tear.

Mr. Jenkins put Liza down and scratched his beard. "Now that you're already wet, you two can be the first to practice the dead man's float."

After Mr. Jenkins finished the swimming lesson, the campers dried off and changed clothes. Then they headed to the dining hall for lunch.

"I wonder what torture the hairy Mr. Jenkins has planned for us now," Eddie said with his mouth full.

Howie gulped down the last of his bologna sandwich. "Maybe he's going to give us lessons on how to yell as loud as a foghorn!"

"Maybe Mr. Jenkins isn't so bad," said Liza. "After all, he did save me."

They didn't have long to wait. "Everybody finish up your lunches and head for the softball field. Let's play ball!" Mr. Jenkins' voice boomed from the corner of the dining hall.

The other counselors headed for the door. But most of the kids took their time.

"Gee," Liza sighed. "Doesn't this guy ever rest?"

Eddie shook his head. "I doubt it. After all, he does have huge circles under his eyes!"

"Besides, werewolves don't sleep at night," Melody murmured to herself.

By the time the campers had finished playing softball, it was late in the afternoon.

"Boy, I'm beat," Liza yawned.

"Me, too," Melody said. "I'll sleep like a rock tonight!"

Howie laughed. "Too bad Eddie's going to sleep *on* a rock tonight!"

"You can't be serious," Melody gasped. "Aren't you afraid of the lone wolf?"

"Of course not," Eddie said as he wiped sweat from his forehead. "Don't worry, I'll sleep like a baby." Eddie didn't talk much during supper or around the campfire that night.

Mr. Jenkins sat in the shadows and began telling the kids about the ways of wolves. "Naming our camp after a wolf is very appropriate. Wolves work together in a pack. They're much like a family. As campers, we should learn from the wolves and work together."

"Aren't wolves mean?" asked one camper.

Mr. Jenkins' black hair swayed above his shoulders as he shook his head. "Wolves have to eat just like you and me. They only prey on animals that aren't able to keep up with others."

"You sure know a lot about wolves, Mr. Jenkins," said Liza.

"Well, you might say I've had some first-hand experience with them," he explained.

"What kind of experience?" Melody asked.

Mr. Jenkins smiled. "Let's just say I've studied wolves."

"But if wolves work together, why did you tell us the legend of the lone wolf?" Howie blurted.

Mr. Jenkins' eyeteeth gleamed when

he grinned. "Last night's story was about an unusual wolf. Perhaps an outcast."

"It could've been a werewolf," suggested Melody. "Maybe that lost boy turned into a werewolf!"

"So you believe in werewolves?" Mr. Jenkins asked. "How very interesting! People in the Middle Ages believed in werewolves, and so did some tribes of American Indians. I guess many people still do believe in them."

Eddie stood up. "I don't believe in werewolves. And I'm going to prove it!"

Mr. Jenkins looked at Eddie. "And how will you prove that?"

"By sleeping outside tonight!"

A hush fell around the campfire as all the kids at Camp Lone Wolf stared at Eddie.

Mr. Jenkins licked his lips before speaking. "Are you sure you want to do that, Eddie? It gets awfully dark out here at night."

Eddie swallowed and hesitated a moment. "I'm not afraid of the dark, and I'm not afraid of wolves because there aren't any around here. It's just a stupid legend somebody made up to scare kids. But it doesn't scare me!"

Mr. Jenkins rubbed the hair on his chin. "You're welcome to sleep outside tonight if you really want to, but make sure you sleep by the fire. . . . That'll help keep the wild animals away."

5

A Cold Night in Camp Lone Wolf

Eddie didn't really think there were any wolves within two thousand miles of Camp Lone Wolf, but he put his sleeping bag next to the fire just in case.

Howie stood close to the fire with Liza and Melody. He threw a twig on the blaze and looked at Eddie. "You don't really have to sleep out here. We all know you're not chicken. Why don't you come inside?"

"Yeah, it's cold tonight." Liza shivered in spite of her blue Bailey School jacket.

"I'm as warm as toast," Eddie said as he snuggled down into the sleeping bag.

Melody pulled the hood up on her jacket. "You'd have to be crazy to want to stay out here—especially after what I saw last night. You ought to sleep inside where you have a perfectly warm, safe bed!"

"I'm safe and warm right where I am," Eddie insisted.

Melody sighed, shaking her head. "Well, you can't say we didn't warn you!"

"It's your funeral." Howie shrugged.

Howie, Liza, and Melody turned and walked toward their cabins.

"Sweet dreams," Liza called to Eddie.

"See you in the morning," Eddie mumbled.

"I hope so," Melody whispered under her breath.

The minute they left, Eddie got colder. It was hard to believe he had been sweating earlier in the day, because now he was so chilled his bones hurt.

"This really is stupid," Eddie grumbled to himself. "There's no reason for me to suffer like this."

"Still planning on sleeping out?" Mr. Jenkins' booming voice made Eddie jump.

"Yes!" Eddie sounded more sure than he felt.

Mr. Jenkins stood a few feet from the fire. "Are you sure you're tough enough to stay out here by yourself? It gets mighty dark in these woods."

"I'm not scared," Eddie said.

Mr. Jenkins smacked his lips and looked at the sky. "The moon's almost full," he growled. "It will make the night a little lighter. But, make sure you have extra firewood—just in case."

"Just in case of what?" Eddie asked.

But Mr. Jenkins had already left. Eddie watched as he disappeared behind a clump of birch trees. The leaves rustled, and then everything became still. It was so quiet Eddie could hear the toilet flushing in Cabin Silver Wolf.

"Afraid of the dark," Eddie muttered. "Whoever heard of such garbage!"

Eddie snuggled into his sleeping bag.

He really was tired. The flames of the campfire died down as Eddie closed his eyes to sleep.

Suddenly the clinking of metal came from the forest. Eddie's eyes popped open in time to see leaves trembling on some nearby bushes.

"Who's there?" Eddie whispered hoarsely.

There was no answer.

"It must be the wind," Eddie muttered. He pulled the sleeping bag up to his chin, but kept his eyes on the bushes. He watched them for what seemed like hours.

All of a sudden, Eddie heard a loud rustling sound. In the eerie glow of the moon, Eddie could've sworn he saw a hairy beast darting through the bushes. It looked too big to be an ordinary wolf.

"Holy Toledo!" Eddie yelped. He dived inside his sleeping bag and waited to be eaten. He mumbled every prayer he knew.

"If you'll just let me live, I promise I'll never beat up on my sister again!"

Then he heard it. A howl that started softly and grew louder until it pierced the night.

"The fire!" Eddie remembered. He scrambled out of his sleeping bag and frantically searched for twigs to throw on the dying fire. His hands got tangled in vines, leaving scratch marks on his skinny arms. Eddie didn't notice because another howl echoed from the bushes. It sounded closer now!

Eddie's hands closed around a bundle of twigs and dry leaves. "This better work," he said as he threw them on the campfire.

Eddie heard another howl as he took a deep breath and blew on the leaves and twigs. But there was still no flame. He blew harder and watched as the twigs caught fire and started burning.

He kept blowing on the burning twigs until the flames jumped high in the air. "You can't get me now!" Eddie yelled into the forest. The howls changed to yelps, then died away.

"Wow! That really worked," Eddie exclaimed. "But I don't know for how long!"

He looked once more at the bushes before he dashed into Cabin Silver Wolf. "Wake up!" he screamed.

A few kids grumbled from under their covers.

"Shut up, we're trying to sleep," Howie mumbled from his bunk.

Eddie bounded up to Howie's bed.

"What d'you think you're doing? Get off of my bunk!" Howie shrieked.

Eddie grabbed Howie by the shoulders. "I heard it!"

"Heard what?" Howie asked.

"The wolf! I heard the werewolf!"

"Maybe in your dreams," Howie grumbled. He hated being woken up.

"Listen, this is for real," Eddie declared. "Didn't you hear it, too?"

"I thought you didn't believe in werewolves!" Howie laughed. Then they both heard the howl of a lone wolf in the distance.

"Now do you believe me?" Eddie said soberly.

6

No Ordinary Wolf

At breakfast the next morning Melody dipped her fork into the soggy scrambled eggs on her plate. "This looks like chicken brains."

"Brains are the least of our worries," Eddie said. "There's a werewolf stalking this camp!"

"You guys are just trying to scare us," Liza insisted. "I don't believe in werewolves."

"Then what did I see last night?" Eddie asked.

"And what did I hear?" Howie turned to Liza.

"It could have been just a regular wolf," Liza said. "After all, we are in the middle of the woods."

"It could have been," Melody said. "But

I saw it, too, and it wasn't an ordinary wolf. It looked more like part wolf and part man."

"A wolfman," Eddie whispered.

"A werewolf," Howie nodded.

"And I'm sure it was wearing dog tags," Melody said softly.

"And I heard something jingling—like dog tags." Eddie agreed.

"It's an army wolf," Liza giggled.

"Maybe," Melody said, "it's Mr. Jenkins."

They all looked at their camp director. He was wolfing down a huge stack of pancakes at a table in the front of the dining hall.

"You'd think he'd never heard of a razor," Melody grumbled. "He's still wearing the same clothes, the same dog tags, and no shoes."

"He may be a slob," Liza said, "but he's not a werewolf. Whoever heard of a werewolf in a kids' summer camp?"

"You hear about crazy people every-where," Howie said. "Why not at summer camp?"

"It's a perfect place for victims," Melody agreed. "Look at all these defenseless kids." The dining hall was filled with sleepy-eyed campers eating their eggs or pancakes.

"Well, we're not going to be victims," Eddie pounded the table. "At least not if I can help it."

"What can you do?" Melody asked.

"I don't know," Eddie admitted.

"I think we should explore Mr. Jenkins' cabin," Howie said. "If we could just get in there, I bet we'd find something we could use."

"You mean, *inside* Mr. Jenkins' cabin?" Liza asked.

"Are you crazy?" Melody asked. "He'd kill us if he found us there."

"That's a chance we'll have to take," Eddie said. "We'll go tonight."

7

In the Wolf's Den

For the rest of the day, Eddie, Howie, Melody, and Liza avoided Mr. Jenkins like poison ivy. When he was teaching archery, they took arts and crafts. When he was in charge of canoeing, they took archery.

"I wonder if an arrow shot through the heart would kill a werewolf?" Melody asked as she missed the bull's-eye with her arrow.

"No," Eddie said. "Werewolves are killed with a silver bullet."

"How do you know?" Liza asked.

"I saw it on the late late show," Eddie said.

"Well, this isn't the movies," Howie said. "So make sure you stay away from

Mr. Jenkins until we can get into his cabin."

After archery practice it was time for dinner. Unfortunately, Mr. Jenkins decided to sit by Melody. The dog tags around his neck clinked when he plopped down on the bench. His hair was matted and his beard almost touched his plate of fried chicken. Melody couldn't help but notice that Mr. Jenkins smelled like a dirty tennis shoe.

"How's camp life?" he growled as he chewed the meat off a chicken leg.

"Uh . . . fine," Melody whispered, edging away from him.

Mr. Jenkins sucked on the meatless bone. "You better eat," Mr. Jenkins said as he cracked the bone with his teeth. "You need to fatten up. There's not enough meat on you to make a good sandwich!"

Melody pushed her plate of fried chicken away. "I guess I'm not very hungry," she whimpered.

"Can't let that food go to waste. I'm so hungry, I could eat an entire chicken— feathers and all," Mr. Jenkins said. He reached over and grabbed a drumstick from her plate.

Melody, Liza, Howie, and Eddie watched as Mr. Jenkins tore the meat from the bone. Then he gnawed on the bone until it was clean.

"Nothing like a good leg," Mr. Jenkins said as he wiped grease from his beard. "You kids better finish dinner. Your cabin counselors are getting ready to teach you how to build a campfire. It's an important skill if you want to survive in the wilderness."

Eddie spoke up. "Why don't *you* teach us?"

Mr. Jenkins scratched his beard and glared at Eddie. "I leave the campfires for others to build. I find the heat a bit uncomfortable." With that, Mr. Jenkins stalked out of the dining hall.

"Did you see how he chewed on that bone?" Melody hissed.

Eddie barely nodded. "And did you notice he's getting much hairier?"

Liza didn't say a word. She was too busy eating the rest of her food.

Mr. Jenkins was nowhere in sight while the cabin counselors taught the campers to build a fire.

"Where do you think he is?" Melody whispered to Eddie.

"I bet he's already out howling. You heard what he said about still being hungry," Eddie said.

"Maybe we better not go to his cabin," Howie whispered. "It might not be safe."

Melody shook her head. "It won't be safe for any of us if we *don't* go."

"Melody's right," Eddie said. "We'll meet back here at midnight. Be sure nobody hears you sneaking out!"

That night, after everyone else had crawled into their beds and gone to sleep, Melody and Liza sneaked out of their cabin. It wasn't long before Howie and Eddie joined them by the ashes of the campfire.

"Now remember," Howie said. "We've got to find something that will save us from werewolves."

Liza shook her head. "You guys are so silly. There aren't any werewolves."

"You might not be so sure once we see the inside of Mr. Jenkins' cabin," Melody said.

The windows in their counselor's cabin were dark as they crept up and peeked inside. Just then the howl of a wolf sounded in the distance. Liza almost jumped on top of Melody. Howie grabbed Eddie's arm.

"I knew he wouldn't be here," Eddie said. "He's the one doing the howling."

"Come on," Melody said bravely. "Let's go inside."

"We're lucky the door's not locked," Howie said as the door creaked open.

It was so dark inside they could hardly see anything. Liza pulled a small flashlight out of her jeans pocket and flashed it around.

Wolf posters hung on the rough wooden walls. The cabin was only large enough for a small dresser, a chair, and the bed.

Books were piled all over the floor. Howie picked one up and gulped.

"What is it?" Melody asked.

Howie's voice shook. "It's called *The Encyclopedia of Wolves and Wolflore*."

"That proves it," Eddie said excitedly. "Mr. Jenkins *is* a werewolf."

"That doesn't prove anything," Liza said as she shone her light on the book. "Maybe he's just a wolf nut."

"He's a nut all right," Eddie agreed. "A werewolf nut!"

"Look," Howie interrupted. "There's a whole chapter on werewolves."

"See, Liza. They do exist," Melody said.

Howie read aloud from the book. " 'Two plants commonly used to cure werewolves are wolfsbane and mistletoe.' "

"Mistletoe!" Eddie snickered. "What're you supposed to do? Kiss 'em to death?"

"I don't know," Howie admitted. "There's a picture of wolfsbane and mistletoe right here. Let's see what it says to do with them."

But Howie didn't get a chance. Just then a wolf howl sounded right outside the cabin door.

8

A Werewolf Cure

"Turn off the flashlight," Eddie whispered.

The four campers stood in total darkness, listening. Outside the cabin, they could hear something sniffing at the door.

"It sounds like a huge animal," Liza shivered.

"With dog tags," Melody said.

There was no mistaking it. They all heard the clinking of metal—and then the doorknob began to rattle!

"Quick," Eddie whispered. "Out the window."

Howie pushed. "I can't get the window open," he gasped.

"Shhh," Melody said. "It's leaving."

And indeed, the doorknob wasn't rattling anymore, and the sniffing noise had stopped. No one said a word as they listened. Whatever had been there was gone.

"I thought we were dead meat," Eddie whispered.

"Me, too," Melody admitted. "Now do you believe there's a werewolf?" she asked Liza.

Liza nodded, her eyes wide.

"And it wears dog tags," Howie said softly.

"There's only one person I know who wears dog tags," Melody whispered.

"Mr. Jenkins," they all said together.

After they sneaked back to their cabins, none of the kids were able to sleep. They were too busy thinking about a werewolf stalking their camp. When they met in the dining hall for breakfast the next morning, they were already tired.

"We've got to get the plants that book

told us about," Eddie said as he nibbled on burned toast.

"But we don't even know what wolfsbane and mistletoe look like," Melody snapped.

"I do," Howie said softly. "I saw the pictures."

"That settles it," Eddie decided. "We're in the middle of the woods. I'm sure we can find mistletoe or wolfsbane."

"But I didn't have time to read about those plants," Howie interrupted. "We don't know what to do with them once we've found them."

"We'll just have to figure it out," Eddie said.

They gobbled down the rest of their breakfast and followed the other campers outside. When they were sure that no one was looking, they all slipped behind a cabin and into the trees.

"How hard can it be to find mistletoe

and wolfsbane?" Eddie asked. "Tell us what it looks like, Howie."

Howie thought for a minute and then said, "Mistletoe has white berries, and wolfsbane has big purple flowers on it."

"Great," Eddie rubbed his hands together excitedly. "We'll find this stuff in no time flat. Then we'll really fix Mr. Jenkins."

"You don't think it'll hurt him, do you?" Liza asked.

"Naw," Eddie said impatiently. "It'll help him be normal again. I bet he hates being a werewolf. For one thing, he can never have a steady girlfriend if he is turning into a werewolf every time there's a full moon."

"Not unless his girlfriend is a she-wolf." Melody giggled.

"Very funny," Eddie said. "Now let's spread out and find this stuff."

Everybody glued their eyes to the ground looking for anything that had white berries or purple flowers. Howie managed to run into a tree, but nobody found any wolfsbane or mistletoe.

"I don't think we're going to find it," Liza complained. "Why don't we go back to the camp and go swimming? It's getting hot."

Melody was ready to agree with Liza when she saw something in a tree. "Look," she shouted. "I think it's mistletoe." She reached up and pulled down a big clump.

"Great," Liza smiled. "Now we can get out of here."

"Not until we find the wolfsbane," Eddie said.

Howie had been out of sight for the last

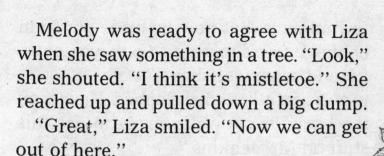

few minutes, but now he came out from behind a tree shouting, "Look, you guys, I found some wolfsbane."

"All right!" Eddie slapped Howie on the back. "Now we're ready to use this stuff on Mr. Jenkins."

"How are you going to use it?" Melody asked.

"You just leave that to me," Eddie said. "I'll take care of everything."

"Fine with me," Liza said quickly. "Just tell me the way back to camp."

"That way," Howie, Melody, and Eddie all said together. Unfortunately they all pointed in different directions.

"Very funny," Liza said. "But which way is it really?"

"Don't tell me we're lost," Melody said.

"We're not lost," Howie said confidently. "I'll show you the way." He started walking, and everyone joined in behind him. They walked a long way but nothing looked familiar.

"We've never passed this rock before," Liza whimpered.

"Now we're really lost," Eddie said as he wiped the sweat from his forehead. "I knew we should have gone my way."

"Well, if you're so smart, why don't you just show us how to get out of here?" Howie's face was red.

"I'll do just that!" Eddie started walking in another direction.

"Wait, Eddie," Melody hissed. "I think I hear something."

They all listened as a clinking sound got closer and closer.

"It's Mr. Jenkins and he's going to eat us up!" Liza cried.

"Don't worry," Eddie said as he picked up a big stick, "werewolves only eat people at night."

"I hope you're right," Liza whispered as Mr. Jenkins broke through the trees. His hairy face and arms made him look like an ape or wild dog. He wore the same clothes and still had no shoes on.

"Why are you kids away from camp?" he boomed.

"We were just out enjoying the woods," Eddie lied.

"We sort of lost our way," Liza admitted.

Mr. Jenkins growled more than he talked. "The first rule of camping is to stay on marked trails. You kids might have been lost out here for days. The wild animals would love to have you for lunch."

"That's what we were afraid of," Melody said.

Mr. Jenkins gave her a dark look and bellowed, "You kids follow me back to camp and don't go out on your own again.

If you want to explore so badly, I'll have to teach you to survive in the woods. A night hike might be the perfect time."

"A night hike?" Liza shrieked.

"Yes, a night hike would be beautiful this time of year. And the moon is full enough for us to see just about everything." Mr. Jenkins scratched hard at his beard, sniffed the air, and then picked a path through the trees. "Make sure you follow me," he growled.

"Now what are we going to do?" Melody whispered.

"We'll have to work fast," Eddie said. "We don't have any time to lose." The four campers silently followed Mr. Jenkins back to camp with their pockets full of mistletoe and wolfsbane.

9

An Unusual Treat

When they got back to camp they headed right for the dining hall. Eddie was so hungry he crammed half a peanut butter sandwich into his mouth.

"How could you think of eating at a time like this?" Melody snapped. "We need to figure out what to do with these plants."

"There'll be plenty of time after lunch for that," Eddie said with his mouth full.

But Eddie was wrong. They barely had time to finish their ice-cream sandwiches before Mr. Jenkins started shouting directions.

"Campers need to know survival skills. So this afternoon we'll go on a learning hike."

Mr. Jenkins tossed backpacks to the campers. "You need to fill your canteen with water and pick up a snack from the kitchen. Meet back here in fifteen minutes."

Melody grabbed Eddie's arm as they walked to the kitchen. "Now what're we going to do? We haven't had time to spread the wolfsbane and mistletoe!"

Eddie jerked his arm away. "Just make sure to bring it with you. I think we'll be safe as long as we carry some."

When everybody was ready, Mr. Jenkins started down the trail. Howie, Eddie, Melody, and Liza followed right behind him. Their pockets bulged with the mistletoe and wolfsbane.

"We're going to hike to a remote area today," Mr. Jenkins yelled over his shoulder. "Very few people even know where it is."

Eddie jabbed Howie in the ribs. "That

means no one will be able to find us!"

Unfortunately, Mr. Jenkins heard Eddie. "You're right. If somebody gets lost, it could be for good. So make sure you stay on the trail. That's the first rule of hiking. The second rule is always hike with a friend."

Mr. Jenkins stopped to face the campers. He scratched his beard before saying, "I expect you to pay attention. You'll need to remember everything I teach you because tomorrow we're going on a night hike." With that he turned and continued up the trail.

Liza felt like her toes were going to fall off by the time they finally stopped to rest. "Whew," she complained. "Hiking is hard."

"It's good for you," Mr. Jenkins growled, scratching his neck. "It'll help get you in shape."

"Mr. Jenkins," Melody blurted. "Where are the bathrooms?"

Mr. Jenkins grinned, showing his eye-teeth. "The bathroom is as close as the nearest tree. Just watch out for poison ivy. It's real bad this time of year."

Mr. Jenkins pointed to the vines growing near several trees.

"No, thanks," Melody said. "I'll wait."

A few kids groaned as Mr. Jenkins led them up a dirt trail. It really was beautiful, with wildflowers filling the spaces between the towering pines.

"Mr. Jenkins, I'm hungry," Liza complained.

"Tough it out a few more minutes. We're almost there."

"Where's there?" Eddie asked.

"You'll see," Mr. Jenkins said. "And when we get there, we'll all have a snack."

"I could eat two humps off a camel," Howie exclaimed.

"I'm too tired to eat," Melody complained.

"You need to eat," Mr. Jenkins boomed. "You could learn from Liza. She has some meat on her bones."

"Did you hear that?" Howie whispered to Eddie.

Eddie nodded his head. "I bet he's planning on eating us during the night hike."

"Poor Liza. He'll probably eat the fat kids first. That's why he wants us to have a snack. He's trying to get us as fat as possible." Howie trembled at the thought.

"Fat or skinny," Eddie said, "it doesn't matter. He'll just eat the fat kids first. Then he'll use us for toothpicks."

"Here we are," Mr. Jenkins called from ahead. "The prettiest spot in this forest."

Directly in front of the hikers was a

cliff as tall as the courthouse in Bailey City. A waterfall tumbled from the cliff and landed in a big, sparkling clear pool.

"Wow," Liza breathed. "This is beautiful."

"It is, isn't it?" Mr. Jenkins said in a surprisingly quiet voice. "This is one reason why I love the woods."

They all gulped down their snacks and waded in the water. Eddie splashed at everyone. By the time he was finished, no one was dry. Playing in the pool was so much fun, no one gave another thought to wolves or werewolves.

After a while, all the campers climbed onto the rocks to dry. Everyone was tired but Eddie.

"Watch this," he whispered to Howie.

Eddie picked up a black hairy spider by one of its legs, then held it close to Liza's blonde hair. Before Liza even had a chance to scream, Eddie dropped the spider. But it didn't go on Liza's hair. It landed right in the center of Mr. Jenkins' huge, outstretched hand.

Eddie gasped. He hadn't seen Mr. Jenkins walk up beside him.

"I see you've found a spider," Mr. Jenkins said.

Eddie's mouth was suddenly dry. "Yeah," was all he managed to say.

"When you live in the woods you learn to eat different things," Mr. Jenkins growled. "As a matter-of-fact, I consider spiders a delicacy. Of course, you have to know which kind won't kill you."

Eddie's eyes grew wide. "Really?"

"Sure. Would you like to eat it?" Mr. Jenkins dangled the spider in front of Eddie.

"No, thanks," Eddie said as he cringed away from the struggling spider.

"Well, if you don't mind, I will." Mr. Jenkins popped the still-wiggling creature

into his mouth and smacked his lips. "Thanks for finding the treat," he said.

Eddie stood rooted to the ground as Mr. Jenkins walked away.

"Did he eat what I think he ate?" Howie gasped.

Eddie nodded. Then, in a voice that Howie could barely hear, Eddie said, "I think we may be in BIG trouble!"

10

Planting a Cure

That night, Melody, Liza, Howie, and Eddie sneaked out of their cabins again. Their pockets were still stuffed with mistletoe and wolfsbane. In the distance, they could hear the howl of the lone wolf.

"Well, at least we know that Mr. Jenkins isn't in his cabin," Eddie whispered.

"Let's hope he stays away long enough for us to hide this stuff," Howie said.

"We better look in that book and see what it says," Melody suggested. "We want to make sure we do it right." They all nodded.

When they got to Mr. Jenkins' cabin Eddie barged right in. He didn't even bother to look in the windows.

"Quick," Liza said as she clicked on

her flashlight. "Find the book."

"I can't," Howie exclaimed. "Everything's been moved."

"Now what do we do?" Melody whined as a wolf's howl echoed through the woods.

"Well, we don't have time to search through all these books," Eddie said. "Let's just spread this stuff around and get out of here."

Each kid pulled out a handful of wilted leaves. Howie opened a drawer in the dresser. "How about if we put some in his clothes?"

"But he never changes his clothes," Liza said. "He's worn the same thing all week."

"He has to change his underwear," Howie said as he dumped the leaves in the drawer.

Eddie took his handful and stuffed it inside Mr. Jenkins' pillowcase. "I better put some under his mattress just to be safe," he said.

"With all his hair, he's got to have a hairbrush," Melody said.

"Here it is." Liza pointed to the dresser.

Melody took the brush and crumbled leaves into it. "Old fur face ought to get a kick out of that!" she laughed.

Only Liza still had her mistletoe left. "I don't know what to do with mine," she complained. "There're no good places left."

"Well, hurry up," Eddie said. "We don't have all night."

Just then, a howl sounded nearby.

"Yikes!" Liza cried, throwing the mistletoe in the air. Little pieces of leaves scattered throughout the room. "Let's get out of here!"

All four kids squeezed through the door at the same time and raced down the dirt path to their cabins.

"That was close," Melody gasped.

Howie nodded. "We finished just in time."

"Let's hope it works," Eddie said gravely.

11

Pussycat

The next morning Mr. Jenkins wasn't at breakfast. As a matter-of-fact, he wasn't anywhere in sight.

"Maybe he vanished like the boy in the legend," Liza whispered.

Eddie shook his head. "I bet he's just resting up for tonight."

One of the other camp counselors interrupted with an announcement. "Mr. Jenkins isn't feeling well this morning. He's suffering from an allergic reaction."

Howie poked Eddie in the ribs. "It's the wolfsbane and mistletoe," he whispered.

Eddie agreed. "If he wasn't a werewolf, he wouldn't be sick."

The camp counselor continued. "Hope-

78

fully, he will be better in time for the night hike."

"Do you mean we still have to go?" Melody asked the counselor.

"Oh, yes," the camp counselor said. "Mr. Jenkins wouldn't want to miss tonight's full moon; he would just die if he didn't get to go."

"We might die if we *do* go," Eddie mumbled.

"While you're hiking with Mr. Jenkins," the camp counselor continued, "we have to clean out the cabins."

"You mean, the other camp counselors won't be coming?" Melody gulped.

"No. Mr. Jenkins said he could handle it by himself," said the camp counselor. "So for the rest of the day, we'll take it easy. We don't want you to be too tired for tonight!"

Howie, Melody, Liza, and Eddie tried all day to think of ways to get out of going. By lunchtime they were worried sick.

"I can't eat a thing," Melody said, holding her soggy taco. "I'm too worried about tonight."

Liza bit into her taco. "You might as well eat now. It may be our last meal!"

Howie agreed. "Yeah, we'd better get some food. We may need our strength for whatever happens tonight."

"Look," Melody whispered. "It's Mr. Jenkins." She pointed to a table at the other side of the dining hall. There sat a very pale Mr. Jenkins.

"That can't be Mr. Jenkins. He isn't hairy," Eddie said, shaking his head.

"But it is," Melody insisted. "Look at the dog tags around his neck."

Mr. Jenkins hardly looked like himself. He wore his dog tags, but now he had on Nike tennis shoes and clean blue jeans. His orange T-shirt was clean, too. His hair was neatly combed and pulled back in a ponytail, and no trace of a beard was left. Indeed, it was hard to believe he'd ever been hairy. Sure, he still had hair on his arms. But even that didn't look as thick.

"Wow, that wolfsbane and mistletoe must've worked." Howie looked amazed.

Liza agreed. "It really must be powerful stuff."

"As long as he's around those plants, we don't have anything to worry about," Howie said. "We'll be safe until we go home tomorrow!"

"We don't have to worry about that night hike, now," Eddie smiled.

"You said it!" Melody agreed. "Mr. Jenkins looks more like a pussycat than a werewolf."

12

Almost Midnight

The night sky was as dark as ink, but the full moon lit the trail with an eerie, silvery glow as the campers followed Mr. Jenkins up the dirt trail.

"I've never seen anything like it," Melody said.

"Nobody can grow hair that fast," Liza agreed.

"Nobody human, that is," Eddie added.

Already, a thick black stubble covered Mr. Jenkins' face. His hair was tangled and even his arms looked hairier.

"The wolfsbane and mistletoe must not affect him when he's away from it for long!" Howie declared.

"If only we'd saved some, maybe we'd have a chance!" Melody wailed and stumbled over a root sticking up in the trail.

"Maybe we could find some more," Eddie said. "After all, we are in the woods."

"No way," Howie moaned. "Remember how long it took us to find it the first time? And that was in broad daylight."

Liza clicked on her little pocket flashlight and said softly, "I still have some left."

"What?" they all cried together.

"I saved some of my mistletoe. I thought I could keep it until Christmas." Liza pulled a very crushed clump of leaves out of the pocket of her jeans.

"Liza, you're fantastic," Eddie said, grabbing it from her hand. "Now we just have to get close to him."

Howie pointed to Mr. Jenkins, who was far ahead on the trail. "That won't be easy. He's getting hairier by the minute."

"I wonder how long it takes him to turn into a werewolf," Melody said.

"It shouldn't be long now," Howie gasped as he looked at his glow-in-the-dark watch. "It's almost midnight. And look—he's taking off his shoes!"

The four campers gasped as Mr. Jenkins untied both Nike tennis shoes and kicked them to the side of the trail.

The other campers didn't notice that Mr. Jenkins was changing in front of their very eyes. Half of the kids looked like they were ready to fall asleep, and the rest were hooting and hollering about being out in the woods so late.

"Come on," Eddie said. "It's up to us to save everybody."

Howie, Liza, Melody, and Eddie ignored the complaints and shoves of the other campers as they pushed their way to the front of the group. Finally, they were right behind Mr. Jenkins.

Eddie used all the skill of a pickpocket as he inched closer. Holding his breath,

he dropped the mistletoe into Mr. Jenkins' open backpack. He didn't dare
breathe until he joined his friends.

"You did it!" Howie whispered as he
patted Eddie on the back.

"I just hope it isn't too late," Eddie
sighed.

13

The Lone Wolf

It wasn't long before Mr. Jenkins started to scratch.

"It's working," Eddie said as he grabbed Howie's arm.

"Thank goodness," Howie cried.

Mr. Jenkins was scratching like a dog with fleas by the time they reached the top of a hill. He turned to face the kids. His eyes looked red and teary. "We'll stop here and rest," he growled.

Everybody dropped to the ground and slipped off their backpacks. Even Mr. Jenkins.

"Oh, no!" Melody exclaimed. "Mr. Jenkins took off his backpack."

"Now what are we going to do?" Liza whined.

Howie tried to stay calm. "As long as he's near the mistletoe, we should be safe."

At that moment Mr. Jenkins stood up. He scratched his beard and announced, "I'm going to scout out the trail ahead. You kids sit tight." With that he walked off into the night leaving his backpack behind.

"We're dead, now," Liza gasped. "Without the mistletoe nearby, he'll turn into a werewolf!"

"There's nothing we can do but stick together," Howie said quietly. "We better tell the rest of the kids about Mr. Jenkins. That way everyone will be prepared."

Melody, Liza, and Eddie nodded. They turned and faced the other campers.

"You're crazy," one of them said when Eddie had finished telling them about Mr. Jenkins.

"Yeah," a little girl in front agreed. "I

don't believe in werewolves. There's no such thing."

"I think you've watched too many movies," said a boy from the back.

"But haven't you noticed how hairy Mr. Jenkins is?" interrupted Melody.

"And he's allergic to plants that are used to cure werewolves," Liza added.

"So, I'm allergic to a lot of plants," a chubby girl with pigtails said. "And I'm not a werewolf."

The rest of the kids started laughing and making fun of Howie, Liza, Eddie, and Melody. They were so busy giggling they didn't notice the clinking sound coming from the trees near the trail.

Then a low growl sounded from the clump of bushes. One by one, the kids got quiet.

"What's that?" Howie whispered.

Nobody answered as the growls grew a little bit louder.

"Maybe it's just a dog," a girl in a red jacket said.

Just then, whatever was in the bushes darted back into the woods. There was enough moonlight to show the glimmer of dog tags.

"That's no dog!" Melody exclaimed. "Dogs don't run on two legs."

"And dogs aren't that big," cried Eddie.

And then they heard it. A howl that started out low. It grew louder and louder until it seemed as if the woods were filled with the cry of the lone wolf.

"It's the werewolf!" Melody yelled. "Run for your lives!"

The campers turned and fled. Even though they were scared, they remembered to stay on the trail. They didn't stop until they were safe in their cabins.

The dining hall was quiet the next morning as all the campers thoughtfully chewed on rubbery sausage. Mr. Jenkins sat at a table all by himself. The black stubble on his face was almost a full beard, and his hair looked like it had pieces of dry leaves and twigs stuck in it. His clothes were torn and dirty. He didn't say a word about the midnight hike.

The bus arrived after breakfast. All the campers dragged their blue Bailey School gym bags onto the bus and found a place to sit down. Eddie and Howie headed toward the back of the bus. Liza and Melody sat right in front of them.

"I'm sure glad camp is over," Liza said.

Several kids sitting nearby nodded.

"We're just lucky to get away before Mr. Jenkins ate us," Howie said.

"Do you *really* believe Mr. Jenkins is a werewolf?" a scrawny boy across the aisle asked.

"You have to admit," Eddie said slowly. "Mr. Jenkins is no ordinary camp director."

The kids on the bus stared at each other. "You could say that again." Melody said.

The campers peered out the window as the bus slowly began to move. There stood Mr. Jenkins. He waved and scratched his beard. Then he took a deep breath and howled the call of the lone wolf.

About the Authors

Debbie Dadey and Marcia Thornton Jones have fun writing stories together. When they both worked at an elementary school in Lexington, Kentucky, Debbie was the school librarian and Marcia was a teacher. During their lunch break in the school cafeteria, they came up with the idea of the Bailey School Kids.

Debbie and her family live in Fort Collins, Colorado. Marcia and her husband still live in Kentucky.